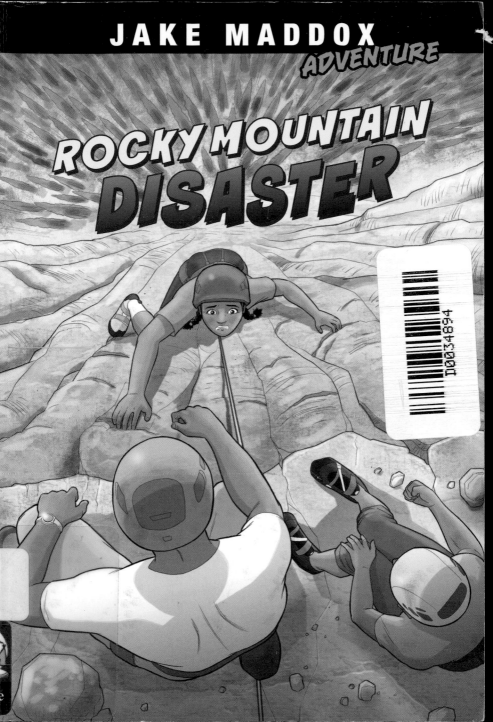

JAKE MADDOX
ADVENTURE

ROCKY MOUNTAIN
DISASTER

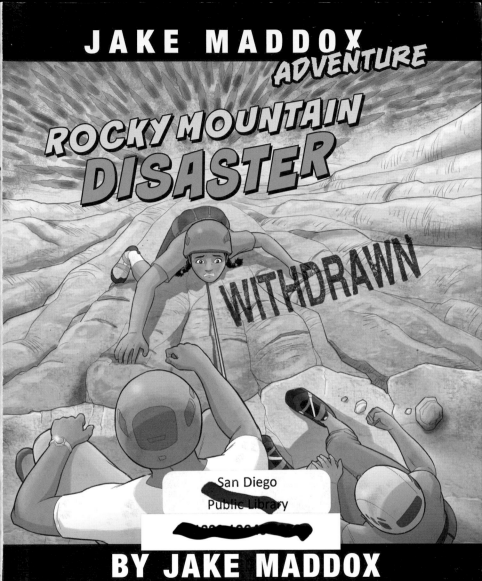

WITHDRAWN

BY JAKE MADDOX

Text by Salima Alikhan
Illustrated by Giuliano Aloisi

STONE ARCH BOOKS
a capstone imprint

Jake Maddox Adventure is published by Stone Arch Books,
an imprint of Capstone.
1710 Roe Crest Drive
North Mankato, Minnesota 56003
www.capstonepub.com

**Library of Congress Cataloging-in-Publication Data is available on
the Library of Congress website.**
ISBN: 978-1-5158-8228-2 (library binding)
ISBN: 978-1-5158-8337-1 (paperback)
ISBN: 978-1-5158-9222-9 (eBook PDF)

Summary: Twelve-year-old Carly has recently recovered from an
illness and to celebrate, Carly, her older brother, Ajay, and their dad
go on a climbing trip in the Rocky Mountains. Even though Carly
tries to convince her family she is a hundred percent better, her
troubling bouts of tiredness give her away. When an unexpected
injury forces Carly and Ajay back down the mountain, Carly's health
is put to the ultimate test.

Designer: Sarah Bennett

Printed and bound in the USA. PO3837

TABLE OF CONTENTS

CHAPTER 1

THERE'S NOTHING LIKE THE MOUNTAINS

"How many constellations can you guys see?" Dad asks Carly and her brother, Ajay, as they roll out the sleeping bags next to their tents.

"I can count five," Ajay brags. "Watch and learn, Carly."

"I can count even more than that," she says. Ajay's only a year older than Carly and acts like he knows everything. But she knows she's right—every time they go on one of their camping adventures with Dad, Carly's the one who spots the most constellations.

Dad settles down on top of his own sleeping bag. Later, when it's time to go to sleep, they'll pull the bags into their tents and turn in for the night.

But right now it's time for stargazing. Dad puts his hands behind his head and sighs. He is content.

Carly knows just how he feels. There's nothing like being in the mountains. Their peaks surround the campsite. She loves the nights before climbs; they're so magical. The stars blaze across the night sky. She can even see parts of the Milky Way.

She lies down too and looks up. Tomorrow, they'll be up on the mountain that looms right in front of them.

"I see the Big Dipper right now," says Dad. "Can either of you see Orion?"

"Right there!" Carly points before Ajay does.

The three stars that make up Orion's belt are bright as can be.

"Zeta, Epsilon, and Delta," Carly says. She points at each star she names.

Dad has been taking Ajay and Carly mountain climbing for years. When the two were really little, they'd just camp and hike in the hills. And then they started going higher and higher as they got older. Now the three are scaling up mountains and cliffs. They have real climbing equipment—harnesses, helmets, special shoes, and more.

There's nothing like getting to the top of a mountain and looking down at the world spread under you, knowing that you made it all the way up there, Carly thinks.

She loves that they're back in Estes Park, Colorado. It's near Rocky Mountain National Park. This was always their favorite park to come to, before Carly got sick.

It's over now, she tells herself firmly. Carly balls up her fists. She hates thinking about what it was like to be sick. Tomorrow is her chance to prove that she feels just as well as anybody else. It's her first big climb since she's been better.

Carly's face turns red just thinking about it. For most of last year, Carly was sick. She was really sick—sick enough to be in the hospital.

Carly didn't know if she'd ever be able to climb again. It was the scariest feeling in the world for her. She's better now, but she doesn't really feel like people are treating her like she's better. She wants things to go back to normal. The way it was before she got sick—before she stayed at the hospital.

Carly takes a deep breath of fresh mountain air. The mountains make it hard to remember that she was ever sick. It feels like a different world out here.

She thinks about how different the stars look in cities, where she can hardly see them because of all the light pollution. And the air in cities doesn't feel nearly as clean. Here, it is crisp and pure.

There's nothing, nothing like being in the mountains. And tomorrow she's going to be a normal climber again.

CHAPTER 2

UP, UP, UP

"Is that everything?" Dad calls the next morning, as he packs the last of his gear into his backpack.

Ajay stuffs his bedroll into his own pack. "Almost everything. Carly, did you get your bedroll? And do you have your helmet?"

"Do you have yours?" Carly asks impatiently. She's been packed for almost an hour. Ajay never used to check up on her this much before she got sick. It's like he thinks she can't do anything by herself. "You don't need to keep treating me like I forgot everything about climbing. I'm the same as I was before."

"Carly, Ajay's just trying to make sure we have everything." Dad sounds annoyed. He hates when the two fight. "And both of you need to grab your helmets."

Getting her helmet, she makes sure it's snug in her backpack and ready for her to grab.

On easy hikes, Dad lets Carly and Ajay wait until they get to a cliff before they put on helmets. But there are a few steep parts to this hike. Their dad will want them to wear their helmets during those parts as well.

Ajay rolls his eyes at Carly as he puts his backpack on. "If you want me to stop treating you like a baby, stop acting like one," he says. "A few months ago, you were still getting dizzy, and half the time, you wouldn't even admit it!"

"Ajay," Dad says sharply, "that's not helping!"

Carly tries not to think about Ajay's words. She doesn't feel dizzy now. She feels strong. Her feet practically itch to get going. The mountain looms up into the clouds, waiting for them. The morning is cold and fresh, and they can smell the pines and the earth.

Carly hasn't climbed this peak before. Dad and Ajay climbed it while she was sick. She had asked to do a higher one, but Dad had told her, "This is a good peak to start with, Carly. If you do OK on this one, we'll do a higher one soon."

Carly sticks her chin up, determined. If she can just make this peak today, she will know once and for all that she's beaten this illness.

Carly checks her phone. "Mom texted to tell us to have fun on the hike," she tells the group.

Carly quickly texts her back: *About to start! Can't wait!* Then she puts her phone in her pack. The group is ready to go!

"Careful," Ajay tells Carly as they start up the mountain onto uneven terrain.

Dad and Ajay watch Carly, but she ignores both of their stares. Her feet are sure and solid with each step in her new hiking boots. Her pack is just the right weight on her back. She is feeling good and is more determined than ever to see this trip through.

The group steps around the high, beautiful pine trees at the base of the mountain. The branches hang thick and low, and the smell is heavenly. Carly watches her boots step over pine needles and rocks and listens to the birds as she hikes.

"Any time it gets to be too much, tell us, Carly," says Dad. "We can come back another time."

"I'm fine," she snaps. Carly walks along even faster now, taking over the lead from her dad.

Dad and Ajay might be worried that her balance won't be good enough to make it up these rocks. But Carly will never let a sickness get her down again. She looks up at the top of the mountain towering far above them. She imagines what it would be like to stand up there and look down on the world.

CHAPTER 3

A WAVE OF TIREDNESS

For a while they hike silently. Carly's favorite part of mountain climbing is getting to be so close to the outside world and seeing things she'd never see otherwise.

Lots of people never look at nature up close, she thinks. *This mountain has been here hundreds of years, maybe thousands. It's seen so many things happen.*

Eventually, the ground gets drier and less green. There are fewer trees and more rocks. The trees that are there aren't the tall ones at the base of the mountain. Up here, they are shorter and brushier, with bristly leaves.

Soon the group will be in what's called the alpine tundra, which is higher up on the mountain. In the alpine tundra, it's almost all rocks and brush and dry ground. There are also cliffs to climb. Carly can't wait to use her equipment again.

For a split second, Carly feels a tiny moment of tiredness—a deep tiredness. The doctor had told her these moments are normal. It passes, and she feels fine again. She peeks over her shoulder. Dad and Ajay didn't notice a thing.

Almost a year ago, Carly suddenly started getting all these symptoms. She had a fever and headaches. She was throwing up a lot. Her hands and feet were cold, and her neck felt stiff.

At first her family thought it was the flu, but then Carly started getting confused and forgetting things. She suddenly hated bright lights. Her parents took her to the hospital.

It turned out she had bacterial meningitis, which is a really serious sickness. It means the membranes, or skin, around the brain and spinal cord are infected. If it's not treated right away, people can die from it.

Carly was lucky. Doctors put her on antibiotics right away to fight the infection. She was in the hospital for a couple of weeks.

But Carly hated being in the hospital. It was scary and boring. She hated lying there doing nothing. She hated being hooked up to an IV. The people around Carly looked at her nervously all the time. Carly could tell they were worried she'd never get better.

Most of all, Carly hated remembering how a few months before, she'd been climbing with Dad and Ajay. In the hospital, she had wondered if she would ever climb again.

"Everything up here is just like it was before," Ajay says.

"Yeah, nothing's changed," Dad agrees.

Carly usually hates thinking about them sharing something this special without her. But right now, she's just glad they're distracted.

She thinks about the day she left the hospital, which was the happiest day of her life. But when Carly got home, she was still dizzy and confused sometimes. And she still felt really weak. She hated her weakness more than anything.

The doctor had told Carly not to push herself to get better—that it would happen when her body was ready. She had to stay on bed rest for a while. But she was determined to make sure everyone knew she had no plans to stay in bed forever.

As soon as the doctor said it was all right, she started walking around the house. Then she tried the yard. Soon, she went up and down the street. Her strength came back.

Her parents finally stopped looking so worried.

A few months later, Carly begged Dad to take her climbing again. After the doctor said it was OK, they went on a few hikes. Then they went up into the hills. But this is the first mountain Carly's done since she got sick.

Carly breathes in the wild, fresh air. For a moment, it's hard to believe she'd ever been sick at all. But then she remembers that wave of tiredness. She pushes it out of her mind. *I'm not going to let that stop me*, she thinks.

CHAPTER 4

SCALING THE CRAG

The group climbs higher and higher. Carly is tense, waiting for the wave of tiredness to come back—but it doesn't. Behind her, Ajay's whistling. Dad has a big smile on his face.

"This is it!" Ajay exclaims.

It's the first cliff—high and majestic. Its sheer wall gleams in the sun.

"We didn't do this one last time, Carly," Ajay says. "We saved it for you."

"Thanks," Carly says. She really is glad they saved this cliff for her. It's gorgeous. It's got lots of crevices. Plenty of places to place the gear.

"Beautiful," says Dad. He's already checking his equipment. "Must be at least eighty feet. You guys ready?"

"This is awesome, Dad," says Ajay. "It's the biggest single-pitch we've done in a while. You think you can do it, Carly? How are you feeling?"

"Of course I can," she fires back but doesn't look at him. "I wouldn't be here if I didn't think I could do it."

"Stop snapping at us, Carly," Dad says. "We just want to make sure you feel up to it."

She rolls her eyes when Ajay sticks his tongue out at her from behind Dad's back. In her opinion, thirteen is way too old to be sticking his tongue out at people.

Ajay and Carly take off their packs and pull out climbing harnesses. Carly is so excited to do this again that she does a little dance first.

They step into their harnesses and make sure each is good and snug. Dad is already tying the rope into his own harness. Ajay picks up the rope, threads it through his belay device, and clips it in to his belay loop. He'll use the belay device to control the climbing rope.

"Ajay, you'll belay me like usual," Dad says.

This means Dad is trusting Ajay to catch him if he falls. It's Ajay's job to control how much slack Dad has on the rope as he takes the lead up the cliff. Ajay checks Dad's knots to make sure they're secure. Dad checks Ajay's belay device to make sure it's secure and that the carabiners are locked.

Carly looks up at the crag, steep and powerful. Climbing and rappelling are her favorite things in the world to do. She watches Dad climb.

"You're doing great, Dad!" she says.

He's a great lead climber. He goes up the cliff first and places the gear as he goes, putting nuts and cams into crevices and cracks in the rock.

The nuts and cams are the tools that climbers attach their ropes to, so that there's something to catch them if they fall. This is called trad climbing—when climbers place gear themselves.

Dad moves higher and higher, placing the gear Carly and Ajay will use when they climb up after him. He takes his time. He's taught his children to be the same way—to look for the perfect cracks to place gear. They learned how to test gear to make sure it'll support their weight.

Ajay feeds slack into the system as Dad goes higher. Finally, he's at the top.

"It's beautiful up here!" Dad calls down to them.

He gets to work setting up an anchor. There are already two bolts in the rock at the top of the cliff, meaning other climbers use this route a lot.

He clips directly into the bolts and uses opposite and opposing quick draws to secure the system. This provides backup if something fails. He unties the main rope once he's secure and feeds it back down to Ajay.

"My turn!" Ajay says. He gets ready to climb.

Now Carly belays Ajay as he climbs, just like Ajay belayed for Dad. Ajay climbs on top rope. This is the rope that Dad just threw down. He doesn't even have to use the gear—he just goes straight up.

"Finally," Carly whispers to herself. It's Carly's turn to go up. Dad belays her from on top of the cliff, taking in slack as she goes up. Carly has what Dad calls one of the hardest jobs ever.

She has to do the "cleaning." That means she stops wherever Dad placed cams and nuts and removes them. Climbing equipment is expensive, so they'll need to get all of their gear back.

As she climbs, the excitement she's always felt on climbs flows through her. Carly had been worried that maybe she wouldn't remember exactly what to do, but now she's glad to see her feet and hands seem to remember where to put her weight.

As Carly removes gear and clips it to her harness, she feels the extra weight she's taking on. The process takes time and is super tiring, but she's so glad Dad thought she could do this that she almost cries.

Then, suddenly, another wave of tiredness comes. Carly pauses.

"What is it, Carly?" Dad shouts down, his voice anxious. "Are you all right?"

She takes a deep breath. The tiredness passes. "Yeah, I'm fine. Just being careful."

"Are you having another spell?" Ajay shouts from above. That's what Carly's family used to call her moments of dizziness and tiredness.

"No," she shouts back stubbornly and keeps moving.

Dad is quiet, and Ajay doesn't believe her. But Carly is almost at the top, and it doesn't take much time for her to pull out the last of the gear and haul herself over the top.

Carly stands next to Dad on the top of the cliff, catching her breath. Dad hugs her for a long time. There are tears in his eyes.

"See? I made it," Carly says.

Dad laughs a little. "I knew you could do it, kiddo. But how do you feel? Really?"

"Fine. You know you don't have to keep asking me that," Carly says.

Carly isn't looking at him. She looks around the ledge instead. It's big enough for all three of them to safely be off belay. "It's safe to unclip."

"You're right," Dad says. "And I'm sorry, Carly, I think I just got in the habit of asking how you were all the time. You know it's very important to tell us when something's wrong, right? I need to trust that you'll do that."

Carly feels guilty as they unclip. She won't say anything that will spoil the climbing trip.

"Awesome," she says instead.

Ajay stands next to Dad and Carly, looking out. The world sprawls out underneath the mountain. They see woods, fields, and far in the distance, roads. But Carly feels as far away from civilization as possible.

Carly notices that the sky is darkening a little bit, and clouds are rolling in. She crosses her fingers that it doesn't start raining.

Dad points upward to the top of the mountain. "What do you say we take a break and eat something before we keep going? And we'll see what those clouds decide to do."

"Good idea. I'm starving." Ajay has his pack off in no time. He roots through it for the food he's brought.

The group sits on top of the cliff and eats cheese, peanuts, and beef jerky, which are their favorite things to eat on trips. As they're finishing up, Dad gets up to move toward the back of the ledge.

"Hey, kids, I think there's a cave back here!" he calls. "Maybe we can do a little exploring before—"

Then Ajay and Carly hear a crunch. Dad shouts, "Whoa!"

Carly leaps to her feet. Dad is slipping on some loose rocks. Before she can make it to him, he's fallen. His face twists with pain.

"What happened?" Ajay cries.

"My ankle." Dad bites his lip. His voice sounds like he's in pain. "I think I broke it."

CHAPTER 5

BACK DOWN

Nothing like this has ever happened on any of their trips before. Of course, they know that climbers get injured all the time. Climbers have to be very careful.

Everyone in their family has all been trained in first aid in case anything happens. But so far, no one has gotten injured. They've always been lucky.

Ajay and Carly sit with Dad as he sees if he can still move his foot. He tries to hobble a few feet, then winces and collapses again. "I can't." Now his face looks sweaty. "I think . . . I think we'll have to call for help."

"We need to wrap your foot first." Carly gets out the first aid kit. Ajay helps her wrap Dad's ankle. Compression is important to keep the swelling down.

"You'll have to elevate your foot," Ajay says.

"No worries, Dad, we'll call Search and Rescue," Carly says. She already has her phone out. She frowns at the screen. "No way. I don't have a signal. Do you, Ajay?"

Ajay and Dad pull their phones out too.

"No reception, either," says Ajay, his face pale.

"Me neither." Dad sighs. "We know reception is bad on the mountain."

"I had it at the campsite!" Carly says. "I was texting Mom."

The three look at each other.

"Carly and I can go back to the campsite and call Search and Rescue," Ajay says.

"I'll rappel back down with you and wait at the bottom of the cliff," Dad says.

The three clip back in and agree that Dad should go down first. The rope is still anchored in, so Dad lowers himself as smoothly as he can. He's slower than usual and lands painfully at the bottom. Carly goes next. At the bottom, she rushes to Dad, who's sitting and watching Ajay come down. Dad's face looks kind of gray.

Carly gets a blanket out of his pack and wraps it around his shoulders. "Wait over there," she orders him, nodding toward a little cave in the cliff face. "Just get right in there and wait for us, in case it starts raining. We'll be right back. And elevate your foot if you can."

Once Ajay gets to the bottom and is out of his harness, he helps Dad hobble to the little cave. It's not much shelter, but it's better than nothing.

"I'm leaving you most of our food," Ajay says, stuffing beef jerky in Dad's bag.

"Keep some of it for yourself," he says. He smiles, but they can tell he feels terrible. His skin feels cold.

Carly feels frustrated and scared, but she knows it's probably the best thing to leave soon. The sooner the two go, the sooner they can get help for Dad.

"OK, Dad." Carly hugs him shakily. So does Ajay. "We'll be right back."

"Be as careful as ever," Dad warns us. "Do not rush just because of my ankle. Our group can't have anyone else getting hurt right now."

Carly looks at Ajay and knows what he's thinking because she's thinking the same: they want to run down the mountain as fast as they can.

"We'll be careful, Dad! Promise," Ajay says.

Ajay and Carly set off down the mountain. They're extra careful to check for loose rock as they move along the stones.

Carly realizes now how scared she is. They've never hiked without Dad before. It's awful thinking of him up there alone and injured.

Sometimes when people break bones, they go into shock, she thinks. *What if Dad goes into shock up here and gets really sick?*

"How long do you think it'll take Search and Rescue to get here?" Carly asks Ajay.

"Depends. I think I remember our mountaineer trainers saying anywhere from an hour to four hours." He frowns and his eyebrows scrunch together.

"I should have gone by myself," Ajay continues. "We don't need you getting hurt too. I know you got tired or dizzy earlier and that you lied to Dad."

Carly's face gets red, and she balls up her fists. The last thing she needs is Ajay tattling on her. She'd never be allowed to go climbing again. "You don't know what you're talking about!"

"Oh, yeah? Look me in the eye and tell me you didn't get dizzy," Ajay says.

Before she can answer, she hears a loud crack up in the sky. A droplet of rain hits her forehead.

"I was hoping that wouldn't happen!" Ajay says. "Just our stupid luck!"

"Quick!" Carly says and rushes toward an outcropping in the rock.

CHAPTER 6

STORM

Ajay and Carly crouch under the outcropping and stare out at the rain. The droplets become a downpour, and suddenly rain is pounding the landscape. Lightning flashes in the sky, and thunder rumbles over the mountain.

"Do you think that cave is enough shelter for Dad?" Carly asks as they pull on their ponchos. It makes her sick to think of Dad trapped up on the ledge during this storm. "He packed a poncho, right?"

"He'll be fine," Ajay says, but he sounds scared too. "He knows what he's doing."

Carly is shivering, but she doesn't notice. She's worried for her dad. It was weird for her to see him look so helpless. All her life, her dad has been the one who's strong. She can't get the image of him lying there out of her mind.

Finally, after about an hour, the rain and thunder stop.

"At least it was a pretty quick storm," Ajay says to her.

Ajay and Carly crawl out from under the outcropping. They start moving back down the mountain. Carly and Ajay constantly remind themselves to be extra careful now. That the rocks are slick from the rain.

The two keep scrambling down, watching their footing. There still aren't many trees here. Carly looks ahead down the slope. There aren't too many places to catch themselves if they slip.

"You ignored me before," Ajay says. "I know you felt dizzy earlier. Or tired. Why didn't you say anything to us?"

Carly starts scrambling even more quickly down the rocky mountainside. "You don't know anything." She's so mad now she can't see straight.

They walk a few more feet before she skids on the rock. Her feet slip out from under her before she realizes what's happening.

Carly lands on her bottom, but she's on an incline. Loose pebbles and stones rain around her. She lets out a yelp as she slides down the slope.

Carly scrambles to grab for a hold. She remembers to flatten herself against the rock, like they've been taught. She manages to keep herself from sliding more than about six feet.

Ajay reaches out for her. "Careful," he says and hauls her up.

Carly gets back onto more solid ground and sits there. She stands shakily but starts walking again. This time, she goes down the slope slowly.

Another loose stone rolls out—but now, it's from under Ajay's feet!

CHAPTER 7

TAKING OVER

Ajay wheels backward, turning and flattening himself as he falls. He lands on his forearm at a weird angle and cries out.

"Ajay!" Carly helps him back up. He yelps as she pulls him up under his arms.

"I landed wrong." He scrambles up and sits down on a boulder. He rocks back and forth as he grabs his wrist. "It's killing me." Carly looks at Ajay's wrist. It's already swelling.

Now Dad and Ajay are injured. The stress of the situation hits Carly. She gets a wave of tiredness she can't ignore. She's suddenly out of breath and sits down on the wet stones.

"We'll make a splint and a sling," she says after she's caught her breath. Carly tries to keep her voice even. The mountaineering guides taught her that panicking when someone is injured makes things worse.

Carly already has her first aid kit out. The group each has their own, which she's grateful for now. She's shaking, but she tries not to let Ajay see.

Carly takes out the materials to make a splint. The most important thing is to immobilize his wrist. She folds the splint, creating strength in it by making a C-curve, then molds it to fit her forearm first.

Once it fits Carly, she applies it to Ajay, adjusting it to his arm. He winces and trembles. Carly uses a bandage from the pack to wrap his arm in the splint.

"I think we should make you a sling too," she says.

If his arm is in a sling, it'll be even harder to move it. This will protect him as he hikes down. Carly takes the piece of fabric out of the kit. She has to pull off Ajay's poncho first. She's glad they have the sleeveless kind.

She places the triangle of fabric under his injured arm and over his uninjured shoulder. She ties the ends of the sling securely and pulls his poncho back over his head.

"It's not perfect," she says. "But I guess it works. Are you OK?"

His face is as sweaty as Dad's was, but at least his arm is secure. "Yeah."

They'll have to be extra careful now. Ajay's balance won't be as good if he can't use both arms. If he goes into shock, Carly will have to leave him behind and go for help, and she really doesn't want to do that.

"I can try to take my pack on my good arm," he says.

"No, that'll throw your balance off even more," Carly says. "We'll have to leave it here."

She's surprised Ajay doesn't argue with her. That shows Carly more than anything else that he doesn't feel well. She goes through his pack and takes out the stuff that's most important—his first aid kit, phone, water, headlamp, matches—and stuffs them into her bag.

Carly stashes his pack behind the boulder and heaves her pack on with a grunt. It's heavier now, but they might need all that stuff. She'll just have to rest if she gets tired.

"Let's check and see if we have reception yet," she says.

Carly looks at her phone and Ajay's. No luck. Neither of them have reception. They keep going, slowly this time. Ajay is sad and frustrated, but he just keeps walking, as carefully as possible. It starts to rain again.

"At least there's no lightning this time," Carly says.

On the really steep parts of the mountain, they get on their bottoms and scoot over the slippery rocks using their hands. Ajay only has one hand to use, of course. Carly wonders if she should keep him talking, to keep his mind off things.

Her chest is tight with worry. *What if I get too tired to help him? What if he falls again?*

She realizes this is maybe how Ajay has felt since she got sick.

"I kind of get why you ask me all the time if I'm OK now," Carly mumbles. "I've been tired today. I didn't tell you guys because I wanted to keep going. Happy?"

"I knew it." Ajay smiles a little, even though he's panting. "It's not that we don't think you can do things. It was just really scary when you were sick."

"I hated being sick," Carly admits. "I felt like I couldn't do anything."

"I'd feel that way too," he says.

"I wanted to make it to the top," she says, "so everyone would stop asking me if I'm all right."

"Well, in this case," Ajay says, "it's just as good that you got us to the *bottom* of the mountain!"

CHAPTER 8

AT THE BOTTOM!

Finally the trees are bigger and closer together. They'll glimpse the campsite in just a few minutes.

Carly is so relieved that she has to force herself to go slowly. She makes Ajay walk in front of her, letting him set their pace. She can also make sure he's OK.

And then, there it is—their campground!

"Thank goodness!" she breathes.

Ajay and Carly take shelter under one of the thickest trees they find. It's barely raining under there.

Carly fishes out her phone. She lets out a whoop when she sees that she has a signal and calls 911.

"Hi, we're climbing, and our dad is injured!" Carly shouts when the operator picks up. "He's still stuck up on the mountain! And my brother's wrist is hurt. We need Search and Rescue."

"OK, can you tell me where you are?" asks the dispatcher.

Carly tells the dispatcher where to find them. Thanks to Dad, Carly knows their campground's exact location. He always makes sure Carly and Ajay know exactly where they are when they camp and climb.

"I'll send a ranger over to you while you wait for Search and Rescue," the operator says, before Carly gets off the phone.

Ajay and Carly huddle under the tree, waiting. Ajay looks paler than before, and he's shaking now.

"I'm dizzy," he admits. "The pain's pretty bad."

Finally, headlights appear in the rain. A park ranger's car drives into the campground.

Carly runs over to the ranger and explains who she is.

The ranger says, "Hop on in, I'll take you back to the ranger station. You can wait for Search and Rescue there. It'll be our local volunteer Search and Rescue, so it may take a little while."

CHAPTER 9

RANGER TO THE RESCUE

Ajay and Carly crawl into the ranger's warm, dry car. They're still drenched and shivering, but it feels great to be warm.

The ranger drives for a little while down a gravel road to a small log cabin. It's the ranger station.

Inside, she gives Carly and Ajay towels to dry off. She heats some tea in the microwave and gives them both mugs.

"How will Search and Rescue get our dad?" Ajay asks in a small voice. Carly's glad he asked. She glances at the clock on the wall of the cabin.

"They will have to go up the mountain with a stretcher and get him down that way too," she says.

Carly and Ajay sit silently after that. They each listen and wait quietly, staring at the phone.

* * * *

A little while later, an ambulance arrives. The EMTs ice and re-wrap Ajay's wrist.

"You did a good job," one of them says to Carly. They quickly finish their wrapping. "This will have to do until we can get you and your brother to a hospital."

"That's fine," says Ajay. "I'm not going anywhere until we know Dad is all right."

Outside, it's stopped raining. It's dark by the time Carly and Ajay finally hear people arrive outside the ranger station. Carly races outside.

"It's Dad!" she screams to Ajay and runs to him.

The EMTs load Carly and Ajay's dad straight into the ambulance, while the kids watch anxiously.

The EMTs let Carly and Ajay clamber up inside to sit beside him. Dad smiles wide when he sees them. His ankle is already in a splint, and he's drenched. *Probably from the rain*, Carly thinks.

"Kids! You're all right!" Dad cries out. He notices Ajay's wrist and nods his head toward it. "What happened?"

"I fell," says Ajay. "Carly splinted it for me on the way back. I guess we're all going to the hospital."

"I'm so glad you're all right, Dad!" Carly says.

"They're real heroes." Dad waves his hand at the Search and Rescue team.

The team is talking to the EMTs and ranger. Dad looks at Ajay and Carly. "And you kids are the heroes too. I'm so glad you made it back safely. I'm sorry this happened. This was supposed to be a fun trip." He looks sad.

"Carly was great, Dad," Ajay says to distract his dad. "She really knew her stuff when I got hurt."

Dad squeezes Carly's hand. "Looks like you're the one taking care of us this time."

Now that Carly knows her dad is safe, she wants to admit what happened on the mountain, but she has a moment of doubt. After a deep breath, the words come out of her mouth.

"I really wanted to make it to the peak," she admits. "That's what heroes do. I didn't want anyone to think I'm weak. But I did feel extra tired during the climb."

Carly sees her dad's face darken. She's so scared he'll be mad and tell her she can never climb again. But Dad is just sad that Carly didn't tell him sooner.

"There's nothing wrong with asking for help, Carly. Getting sick doesn't mean you're weak." He tousles her wet hair. "Sometimes accepting help is the strongest thing to do."

Ajay shuffles closer to Dad and Carly. "Plus, look what you did do. You basically rescued both of us," he says.

Carly has never heard Ajay praise her like that. She gapes at him.

"Thanks," she says at last. Carly realizes that just because her family wants to help her, it doesn't mean they think she's a weakling.

"As soon as we're all feeling better, we'll have to come back here," Dad croaks. The ambulance starts to make its way to the hospital.

"And now we know Carly will take care of us if anything happens," Ajay adds.

"You were extra challenging this time," she says to her dad. "But I guess I'll keep you around."

"What about me?" Ajay pipes up.

"I guess that means you too," Carly adds. "If you admit that I would've made it to the top first."

They both laugh.

AUTHOR BIO

Salima Alikhan has been a freelance writer and illustrator for fourteen years. She lives in Austin, Texas, where she writes and illustrates children's books. Her book *Emmi in the City: A Great Chicago Fire Survival Story* was published in 2019 as part of Capstone's Girls Survive series. Salima also teaches creative writing at St. Edward's University and English at Austin Community College. Her books and art can be found online at www.salimaalikhan.net.

ILLUSTRATOR BIO

After graduating from the Institute for Cinema and Television in Rome, Italy, in 1995, Giuliano Aloisi began working as an animator, layout artist, and storyboard artist on several series and games for RAI TV. He went on to illustrate for the comic magazine *Lupo Alberto* and for *Cuore*, a satirical weekly magazine. Giuliano continues to work as an animator and illustrator for advertising companies and educational publishers.